No More

Tears

Also by Tina D.C. Hayes

ROCK CANDY ROMANTIC SUSPENSE
Nefarious

PETAL PUSHERS MYSTERY SERIES
Poison, Perennials, and a Poltergeist
Secrets, Snapdragons, and a Spirit

No More Tears

Tina D. C. Hayes

Hazy Moon Ink

Cover art painted by Jan Cole
Photography by Brittany Hayes

ISBN-13: 978-0692334867
ISBN-10: 0692334866

Hazy Moon Ink

This book is lovingly dedicated to my grandparents, all of whom have battled cancer: Thomas and Nancy Cole, and Bobby and Edna E. Brown.

And to Ramses, my German shepherd angel, who taught me not to give in to grief before its time.

CHAPTER ONE

*The boundaries which divide Life from Death
are at best shadowy and vague. Who shall say
where the one ends, and where the other
begins?*
~ Edgar Allen Poe

September 20th,
Mercy United Hospital, 5:12 p.m.

Rays of sunshine streamed through the window in the hospital lounge, giving the false impression of a cheery world filled with hope. Lisa stared at a stain on the carpet, unable to understand how the planet spun on its axis while her world crumbled apart.

Even though her family filled the room, Lisa had never felt more alone. Her sister Dana lay dying in a hospital bed down the hall. Accepting the inevitable didn't make things any easier.

Her nephew Marcus sat across from her, between his father and his cousin Megan. Lisa's heart went out to the nineteen-year-old boy who looked so much younger just now. From the set of his jaw and his quivering lip, she could tell he was trying his best not to break down in tears again.

Megan patted Marcus on the shoulder before she crossed the room to take a seat beside her mother. Her mouth opened as if to speak, then closed. She took Lisa's hand instead. The two women focused their joint gaze on an insignificant smudge near their feet.

After a few minutes spent in silent hell, Megan spoke, her voice not much louder than a whisper. "Can I get you anything, Mom? Coffee maybe, some water?"

The cafeteria had become a sanctuary for them to escape to when the air in the cancer wing grew too thick with hopelessness. No one particularly liked the mediocre food, but pushing fish sticks around a plate gave the illusion of doing something normal. Anything was better than sitting on deathwatch.

"No. But thanks." Lisa glanced at the clock on the wall, its hands moving in perpetual slow motion. Time itself seemed ridiculous now. She wondered how much longer her own mother would be, but dreaded the signal her return would bring.

CHAPTER TWO

We understand death for the first time when he
puts his hand upon one whom we love.
~ Madame de Stael

Dana steered her car to a secluded area in the city park and turned off the engine. She'd been driving home, but after running a stop sign, decided to pull over until she got herself together. The cluster of buttery yellow daffodils blooming beneath the trees caught her eye, a surreal symbol that everything else in the world was normal.

Her mind reeled, unable to comprehend the things her doctor had told her less than an hour before. She went to his office expecting a prescription for flu medication, for God's sake, not this. Anything but this.

Her temperature and blood pressure were normal, the nurse had told the doctor when he joined them in an exam room that smelled like alcohol and Band-Aids. He listened to Dana's chest through a stethoscope, then sent her for x-rays to check for pneumonia.

An hour later, she'd sat in the doctor's private office and watched him point to backlit pictures of her insides.

"Yes, Mrs. Yager, I did say tumors," he'd answered. "But we won't know for sure whether they are benign or malignant until you have a biopsy." He handed her a slip of paper with appointment information on it. "Dr. Tolbert is the best oncologist in this part of the state."

"I wish I had pneumonia," Dana said, dumbfounded, trying to grasp the situation.

She'd left the doctor's office in a daze and walked through the lobby, ignoring the receptionist who wished her a pleasant afternoon. Her body had operated on autopilot as she drove out of the parking lot.

She picked up the appointment slip from the

seat beside her. The paper rustled in her shaking hand. In a few days, she'd see an oncologist to find out if she had cancer.

Everything was spinning out of control. Dana opened the door and leaned out. Dappled sunshine poured through the branches of the oak tree overhead as she heaved and gagged. The daffodils beside the car dripped with vomit, an anomaly on this otherwise beautiful spring day.

∞

The following Tuesday, Dana sat in front of the oncologist's mahogany desk waiting for her test results. Keith held her hand while Lisa sat quietly in the chair to her right.

The phone call from Dana a few days earlier had been the last thing Lisa expected. There simply had to be some sort of mistake. The lab could have mixed up the x-rays, or maybe her doctor was a moron.

Doctor Abner Tolbert entered his office and closed the door behind him. Seated behind his massive desk, he took a pen from behind his ear, opened the file on the blotter in front of him, and greeted the nervous trio. His spectacles rested near the end of his nose as he peered through their half-moon lenses.

Lisa took a deep breath and offered a silent prayer. Please God, let the dark spots on Dana's x-ray turn out to be some sort of harmless cyst, or better yet, a smear caused by defective medical equipment. She still hadn't exhaled when the doctor spoke.

"I'm afraid I have some bad news, Mrs. Yager." Dr. Tolbert's voice was kind, his eyes shining with compassion as he broke the news. "You have lung cancer."

The room turned into a silent vacuum of spiraling despair. Keith put his arm around Dana, as if to protect her from the disease coursing through her body. Lisa willed herself not to cry; she could not look at her sister.

Dr. Tolbert withdrew Dana's test results from the file and explained the MRI before moving on to the biopsy findings. He paused now and then to translate medical jargon into terms his shaken audience could understand. "The cancer cells are not confined to your lungs," he said, "but have already spread through your torso."

Dr. Tolbert handed his patient a tissue, since tears trickled down her face.

"Thank you," Dana said, defeat etched on her features as she took the Kleenex. She wiped her tears and blew her nose. "Please, go on. I'm fine."

"You have small cell lung cancer, or SCLC," Dr. Tolbert explained. "This type is more aggressive and spreads quickly." He handed them some pamphlets on the subject, then skimmed back over his notes while giving them a chance to think.

After a few moments of intensive reading, Dana looked up, her eyes wide and childlike. "It says there are two stages for this, limited and extensive." She seemed to plead telepathically with her physician before she could go on. "Which one am I?"

The pamphlet clutched in Dana's hand was turned to a page that described these stages, extensive stage being the worst of the two. Lisa had already read over that particular section, and with the information from the MRI, she was fairly certain what the answer would be.

Her fingers dug into the upholstery as she steeled herself for Dr. Tolbert's reply.

"Since the cancer has spread outside the lungs, you're in the extensive stage-"

"But I don't even smoke! Are you sure?" Dana shook her head, her face now whiter than the tissue crumpled in her fist.

"I'm sorry, Mrs. Yager."

"Okay," Keith said. The arm he draped over his wife's shoulder started to shake. "So what can we do about it? Chemo, drugs?"

"Some patients do choose to have chemotherapy." More pamphlets came from the doctor's desk drawer. "Most in this stage opt for radiation, as a palliative therapy."

Lisa found something about the doctor's tone disturbing, as if he had more to say but chose not to. Cold nausea crept from her stomach and slithered up her spine.

"What, exactly, does palliative mean?" Keith asked. Dana placed her hand on his arm.

"It would lessen the symptoms somewhat. Improve her quality of life."

With her gaze fixed on the edge of the desk, Dana sat up taller and squared her shoulders, a straight spine replacing her slouch. "May I have a word with the doctor, in private?" Seeming to sense that Lisa was about to insist on staying at her side, she added, determined, "Please."

Keith and Lisa had no choice but to leave the room. They exchanged dumbfounded, anguished glances in the hall, then she asked him if he was all right.

"Yeah . . . you?" He walked over to the window and peered through the glass before she had a chance to answer.

Lisa leaned against the wall, willed herself to hold it together, and swallowed hard to keep from throwing up. The last thing Dana needed right now was to come out and find them curled up in the fetal position blubbering like babies. She knew in her gut that her sister was in the next room asking how much time she had left.

There must be something she could do to help. There had to be. Lisa couldn't remember a time before she took care of Dana. Their father had died in a car accident when they were very young, which forced their mother to take a second job. Since Sharon had to work long hours and was unable to return home until suppertime, she'd given Lisa the duty of watching over her little sister after school and on Saturday mornings. Although Lisa was only four years older, she had taken the responsibility very seriously. She'd even held her hand when they crossed the street to the library, until Dana turned ten and begged their mom to make her stop.

Flipping frantically through one of the pamphlets, Lisa found the page with detailed information about the stages and scanned through the following paragraphs.

"Oh my God," she whispered, drawing Keith's attention. When he walked over to try to comfort his sister-in-law, all she could do was point at five horrific words: four months to a year.

The doorknob rattled, alerting them that Dana was about to enter the hall. They both feigned fascination with the painting of a bowl of fruit that hung on the wall opposite the door.

In silence, the three headed toward the exit.

"Excuse me. I need to go to the bathroom," Lisa lied. "I'll meet you in the car in a minute."

She doubled back in time to find the doctor in the hall talking to one of the nurses.

"Can I have a word with you, please?"

"Certainly." Dr. Tolbert didn't appear to be surprised to see her again. "What can I do for you?"

"I know you're probably not supposed to tell me, but . . . if you could just give me some idea of . . . how long . . . ." Mad at herself for stammering like an idiot, Lisa wiped her damp face and continued, looking the physician straight in the eyes. "Should we plan for a nice Christmas this year?"

December was eight months away. She hoped the question was vague enough not to encroach on doctor-patient confidentiality.

Dr. Tolbert placed a sympathetic hand on Lisa's shoulder before he answered, his voice soft and compassionate. "I think we should live each day like a holiday, and appreciate how special each and every moment actually is."

Lisa ran to the ladies' room. She latched the stall's flimsy closure and fell back on the toilet seat, sobbing, unable to contain her grief any longer.

CHAPTER THREE

To himself everyone is immortal;
he may know that he is going to die,
but he can never know that he is dead.
~Samuel Butler

Dana decided to organize things while she still had time. All her years as a housewife and stay-at-home mom had strengthened her a pragmatic approach to dealing with difficult situations, a skill that would come in handy while she made important decisions in the coming weeks and months.

Dana scrubbed and organized her already immaculate home until there was nothing left to do, every drawer decluttered, no dust bunnies hiding under the furniture. The housework proved therapeutic, a reason to get out of bed and do something other than feel sorry for herself. Elbow deep in brown suds, listening to Beethoven's "Moonlight Sonata" as she scrubbed scum off the linoleum where the refrigerator usually stood, it was hard to believe her world was ending.

A few days after her diagnosis she checked her life insurance policy, which should cover her funeral expenses but probably wouldn't pay for the headstone. Next, she looked over her health policy, thankful to find out the big 'C' was one of the terminal diseases on which her coverage would pay a large percentage. She called the insurance company several times with questions about how much they paid toward different treatment options, doctor visits, hospital stays, and prescriptions. A wave of guilt crashed over her when she realized Keith would be left with the burden of paying for healthcare that could do nothing to help her.

Her acting skills improved as she struggled to control her emotions around her family. She did *not* want them to feel sorry for her. She tried to put up a strong front, and despite her loathing of anything remotely resembling self-pity, she experienced frequent meltdowns following that April afternoon when the doctor sentenced her to death by cancer.

At home alone, Dana sobbed on the couch, grieving not so much for herself, but for the family she wouldn't be around to care for. She didn't want to leave Marcus without a mother. She wouldn't be there to grow old with Keith. She worried about what would happen to Lisa without her around for companionship, and she felt guilty for abandoning her mother during her golden years.

And sometimes, she would cry simply because she *did not* want to die.

One afternoon she went grocery shopping, her problems forgotten as she strolled through the produce department, down the spice aisle, and into the bakery section, which lured her with the scent of fresh baked bread and a luscious cupcake display.

She was in a good mood on the drive home and hummed along with the radio, until she passed a dead squirrel lying on the side of the road.

Tears dripped onto the steering wheel. The lifeless squirrel's image choked her heart with the ugly reality of impending death.

"Poor, stupid, dead damn squirrel," she wailed, her face contorted in a mask of despair.

The creature—dead, alone, and forgotten in the dirt by the roadside—reminded her that she would suffer a similar fate in a few short months.

"It's not goddamn fair!" She fought the urge to do a U-turn and bury the poor animal, to spare others from the terrifying expression on his cold little face.

❧

"Are you sure that's what you really want to do?" Lisa asked, glad Dana couldn't see her revulsion over the telephone. "I don't think planning your own funeral right now is such a good idea."

Though she dreaded it with every fiber of her being, Lisa agreed to go along for moral support. She wanted to make things easier on Dana, but hoped she wouldn't ask for much input.

Lisa braced herself with a shot of bourbon before their first trip to town. The macabre experience of watching her baby sister pick out her own coffin was hell, pure and simple. She forced a stoic expression and never left Dana's side.

"I like this ivory lining," Dana said, standing in front of one of the open caskets. The salesman encouraged them to handle the display models, to feel the textures of the fabric and the fine wood finish. Dana did just that, gliding her fingertips over the silky smooth interior, picking up a small pillow and rubbing it against her cheek. "What do you think?"

I think I want to get the hell out of here and burn this place to the ground, Lisa thought, chewing the inside of her cheek to keep from saying it out loud. But, obligated to give her honest opinion, she forced herself to answer. "That color washes out your skin tone, makes you look too pale. The dark pink lining in that other one goes better with your fair complexion."

After an hour of walking amongst rows of

caskets, Dana made her selection. Lisa gulped down Tylenol at the water fountain while Dana filled out the order form.

Lunch with Larry came next on the agenda. He and Dana had both attended Mrs. Johnston's sophomore geometry class years before, which made them little more than high school acquaintances.

"I don't think you've met my sister, Lisa Elkins." Dana gestured in her direction when their guest joined them, his oversized stomach wrinkling the blue tablecloth as he squeezed into his side of the booth. "Lisa, this is Larry Baxter. He's a minister at the non-denominational church across town."

Lisa picked at her chicken-fried steak. She had never sat through a more uncomfortable, unappetizing meal in her entire life. Listening to their conversation about funeral plans over mashed potatoes and gravy wasn't an easy thing to do. How could Dana could sit there so calmly and discuss her imminent death with this man she barely knew?

Dana wasn't much of a churchgoer and didn't want the service to come off sounding like a sermon. She explained the unconventional plans she had in mind, sort of a celebration of the life she'd be leaving behind, full of happy memories and reminiscences. Larry talked her into including the twenty-third Psalm, but agreed to do things the way she wanted.

As if those two experiences weren't unsettling enough, nothing could have prepared Lisa for the following day. Dana, ever the perfectionist, seemed to look forward to their destination as she drove across town. Lisa fantasized about jumping out of the moving car, certain that being crushed to death between the asphalt and tires would be a more enjoyable way to spend the afternoon. It was a good thing their mother hadn't come along; she knew Sharon Purcell would have fainted dead away when they pulled up to Murphy's Funeral Home.

They walked through the front door of the establishment, greeted by organ music piped in through clandestine speakers scattered around the building. Lisa didn't know whether to cry or strangle someone when a closed coffin, undoubtedly loaded down with its corpse cargo—probably nestled in the same type of ivory poly-silk lining they'd handled the day before—was wheeled past them.

Dana reached out and took Lisa's hand, a familiar gesture from their childhood when the younger sister depended on the older one to protect her from dangers both real and imagined.

The funeral director, Vernon Murphy, introduced himself and ushered them inside his office. His annoyingly soft voice dripped synthetic comfort. Lisa wondered if he'd missed his calling to be a used car salesman. He handed his customer glossy brochures and proceeded to highlight everything Murphy's Funeral Home had to offer. She plastered an expression on her face she hoped would pass for interest in his spiel. To stop herself from bolting from the building of bereavement, she focused her attention on the wallpaper behind Murphy's head.

A tour through the funeral parlor became the sickening zenith of Lisa's day. Apparently, they kept one room set up for such visits, a veritable diorama of death in this emporium of mourning. At least the coffin on display was empty. Mr. Murphy pointed out where the clergyman usually stood during the service. The new sage upholstery on the seats offered the utmost in comfort, he assured them, showing them first the general seating, then the special row reserved in the front left section for the pallbearers.

"So this is where the family sits," Dana repeated. She tried out a chair in the front, then peered around the room from a mourner's perspective. A large empty frame adorned the ornate table to the right of the podium. Her gaze lingered there, an expression of deep thought etched across her face.

Mr. Murphy noticed what held his customer's attention and spoke, his deep voice oozing serenity. "Often times, the family likes to display photos of the deceased. Some also bring mementoes. Diplomas, war decorations, awards, and the like. Loved ones like to look at the pictures during the ceremony, as it helps them reflect on a happier time in the dearly departed's life."

"I see." Dana appeared satisfied and relaxed. "Very nice. I think I like that idea."

Lisa shivered. The whole scene was too reminiscent of Ebenezer Scrooge meeting the Ghost of Christmas Yet to Come.

Dana turned to the funeral director before she left. "I'll come back in a few days with a list of music I'd like played at my service. And a few other details."

Back in the car, Lisa had to ask, "What did you mean when you said 'other details'?"

"Well, if I told you that," Dana replied, sounding as if she were planning a birthday party for a toddler, "it wouldn't be a surprise."

"Oh God." Lisa rolled her eyes. "I don't even want to know."

❧

A few days later, they went on a shopping trip for funeral dresses. Thankful for the cocktails she'd downed during lunch, Lisa helped her sister pick out the clothes she would eventually be buried in. She did not understand how Dana could remain so cheerful while she paraded around the dressing room in a navy suit and pink blouse, an outfit she'd wear through all eternity, six feet under the ground.

Lisa felt like a royal ass, but agreed to try on the dresses Dana handed her. She had absolutely no desire to buy anything new just now, least of all funeral attire. As she unfastened the buttons on one such garment, Dana passed another outfit under the dressing room door.

"You've got to try this one on, Lis," Dana insisted.

"Fine." Not until Lisa slipped it over her head and listened to the hum of the zipper did she notice what she'd been duped into. She jerked the door open and asked, amusement playing on the edge of her voice, "What the hell am I wearing?"

"You've got to try it with the hat. Here." Dana slammed a hideous orange hat—which did, indeed, match the trim on the tacky chartreuse dress—on top of Lisa's head.

A passing sales clerk paused to ask if they needed any help, but, after seeing what Lisa had on, she made a face and hurried off in the other direction.

Lisa arched an eyebrow when she caught sight of her reflection, her nose turned up at the ridiculous layers of scratchy lace and awful colors. Dana stood beside her, shaking, her hand covering her mouth below an expression of forced composure.

"This is the ugliest-assed outfit I've ever seen in my life. *Nooooo* way." The floppy hat wobbled and nearly fell off as she shook her head in protest. "Oh. My. God. This looks like a Victorian maxi pad. No, even worse, Medusa's tampon. I look like Medusa's freakin' tampon, *if* she had the galloping clap."

Their eyes met in the mirror, and they both burst into the first real laughter either had experienced in weeks.

Later, stopped at a red light on their drive home, Dana took a deep breath and asked a favor. "I want you to promise me that you'll always be there for Marcus. You're like a second mom to him, and you already watch out for him the same way you do with Megan. And for me."

Caught off guard, Lisa turned to peer into

her sister's eyes, soft brown like her own. She wasn't willing to visualize life without Dana yet, not for herself and certainly not for Marcus.

"It will just make me feel better if you promise to take care of him for me . . . after I'm gone."

Lisa swallowed hard, then pinched her leg to stop the flood threatening to overflow her eyeballs. "Don't worry about a thing." Dana touched her hand, which caused a teardrop to trickle down Lisa's face. "I promise."

The light turned green, ending the discussion.

CHAPTER FOUR

No one can confidently say
that he will still be living tomorrow.
~ Euripides

Insomnia plagued Lisa's nights. Disturbing images tormented her mind each time her head touched the pillowcase. The thought of Dana waking up in her handpicked coffin was unbearable. She knew that after embalming— one subject she absolutely refused to let her mind linger on—there was no way anyone could be alive after burial, not in this day and age. Still, on more than one occasion these thoughts sent Lisa running to the bathroom, physically ill.

She had issues concerning the flower sprays

she'd seen so many times, the sweet little bouquets pinned inside the coffin lining, on display above the face of the deceased. Lisa obsessed over whether or not the funeral director moved the flowers before he sealed the coffin lid shut. She'd never seen anyone remove them, but then again, she wasn't in the habit of staring inside the casket after the funeral ended. It sickened her to think Dana might spend the rest of eternity with rotting flowers stuck in her face.

Dana wouldn't have a blanket to keep her warm, down there in the tomb that would soon be hers. Cold natured her whole life, her sister wore thick socks to bed even during the summer. How could Dana spend perpetuity down there in the cold ground, uncovered?

The things that haunted Lisa were trivial. Her sister wouldn't be able to feel the cold, nor would she awaken from the eternal slumber that would come all too soon. Lisa knew it shouldn't make any difference where they placed the stupid flowers.

Dana would be dead.

Nothing would ever matter again.

❧

One afternoon, Dana dropped in to visit. They drank coffee, talking about everything but nothing in particular as they watched their favorite soap opera. Lisa flipped through the channels during the station break, pausing at a repeat of a Christmas episode from some long-canceled sitcom.

Dana's lip began to quiver. The silliest things triggered emotional outbursts. When she'd planned her funeral, she'd been determined to get all the details sorted out, never once letting the morbid aspect of what she was doing get to her. Now, out of the blue, watching someone flash across the television screen in a Santa suit made her squall like a baby.

Startled, Lisa flipped back to their soaps. "Sorry, I don't think we missed anything. See, it's not back on yet." It was obvious the tears had nothing to do with the television program. "What's wrong?"

"Nothing. I'm just being st-stupid." Dana wiped her eyes, irritated at herself for breaking down in front of her sister.

"You're not stupid," Lisa said, "but you're going to be sorry if you don't talk to me. Now, spill it. What's the matter?"

"I'm just feeling sorry for myself. Because . . . because I'm not . . ." she said, crying even harder, ". . . not going to be here for Christmas." She put her face in her hands and wailed. This was the only time she'd broken down in front of anyone since the diagnosis two weeks before. She didn't want to burden Lisa with this, but, as much as she hated to admit it, she needed to let her feelings out.

"Of course you'll be here for the holidays." Lisa reached for her sister's hand.

"No, I won't!" Dana yelled. "Let's face it. I'll be lucky if I stick around until Halloween." She got up and walked to the living room window.

"Don't say that."

"I'm going to die," Dana said, as if to convince herself as well as Lisa. Her fist clutched at the hem of her blouse. "We both know I'll be dead by Thanksgiving."

"You haven't even started treatment yet. Try to be positive-"

"I have cancer, I'm coughing all the time, I feel like hell but I try not to show it." She felt her cheeks flush when she turned to face Lisa. "My chest hurts sometimes. I know I'm dying. I feel helpless, and pissed off . . . because it's just not fair!"

She threw her empty coffee cup against the wall. Broken bits of stoneware scattered across the carpet.

Ashamed of her outburst, she whispered "I'm sorry" before stooping down to gather up the pieces.

"Forget about the damn mug." Lisa stepped between her and the mess. "It's okay. Just sit down and talk to me. I can't do much, but I can listen."

"The last thing I wanted to do was lay this crap on you," Dana said through sniffles.

"That's what I'm here for. It's not good for you to keep your emotions all bottled up."

"You know that's not my style, Lis. I just can't run around like 'oh, look at me. Poor me, with the goddamn cancer.'"

"Well, maybe you should." She passed Dana a box of tissues from the end table. "You're going to have to let us help you through this."

"I know. I just feel so hopeless and useless. And I'm scared to death." Dana reached over to embrace her sister. The floodgates opened and she sobbed on Lisa's shoulder as Lisa cried onto hers. They stayed in each other's arms for a while before breaking apart, both red eyed but calmer after purging some of their pent up grief and anxiety.

"There are so many things I've always planned on doing that just aren't going to happen now," Dana said, sniffling a bit more. "I'll never go to Europe. Probably a good thing, since I only speak English. I'll never win the lottery, go skydiving, or ride in a hot air balloon. But the thing I hate the most, though, is that I won't get to see my own grandchildren, if Marcus ever decides to have any.

"I'm only thirty-nine years old, but my time is as good as over."

CHAPTER FIVE

Thou know'st 'tis common; all that lives must die,
Passing through nature to eternity.
~Shakespeare, *Hamlet*

Three weeks after the diagnosis of small cell lung cancer in Dr. Tolbert's office, Dana began treatment. She had decided against chemotherapy almost immediately. With such a short life expectancy, it seemed ridiculous to spend the time she had left undergoing torturous treatments that would only make her feel worse. Had her cancer been a more treatable kind—a type with a possibility of her recovering to live happily ever after—she would have gladly taken the chemo. Experimental drugs were out, as well. Since doctors measured results over a period of months or years, she wouldn't live long enough to be useful to a study.

The radiation she underwent served more as therapy rather than treatment. The palliative effects were intended to ease the pain growing ever sharper in her chest and along the length of her spine. She hoped the radiation might zap a few tumors while it focused on her bones, though she doubted it or anything else would make much difference to her declining health. When the doctor steered her away from chemo, toward something that would give her a 'better quality of life', a tombstone didn't have to hit her over the head to make her understand what he meant.

The treatments weren't as bad as she'd feared. It reminded Dana of going to a sci-fi tanning bed, one that left her with nuked insides instead of a nice summer glow. At first, the skin on her chest and back became dry and itchy. After the second visit, what felt like a sunburn from hell spread over most of her torso. She didn't complain, although she did ask Keith to rub aloe vera lotion over her raw, lobster red skin.

Fatigue and weight loss were other side effects Dana endured, though they didn't bother her nearly as much as the burns. She thought it was ironic that the more she lay around doing nothing, the skinnier she became. She joked with Lisa—who forced an unenthused half smile—that she wished she could've nuked herself a few years earlier, when she'd tried to shed a few pounds.

While still not her cheery former self, Dana had been in much better spirits since the day she cried all over Lisa's shoulders. Getting the pent up worry and frustration out of her system had lightened her load a bit. She knew the outcome would still be the same, but it seemed less terrifying now.

ലയ

One afternoon toward the end of May, Lisa flopped down on her couch after a long, boring day at work. She'd shown six houses to two clients and her feet ached. The best thing about her job as a real estate agent was that she could pretty much set her own hours, a convenient perk now that she needed extra time off to spend with Dana.

She kicked off her shoes and fumbled with the remote. Days like this reminded her how lucky she was to be divorced. The only dinner she planned to cook tonight was a frozen pizza, unless she dozed off before she made herself get up and put it in the oven. Megan's deadbeat dad had left to 'find himself' a couple years into the marriage and might as well have fallen off the face of the earth.

Just as she found a show to watch, a Lifetime movie with a gorgeous leading man, her telephone rang.

For some odd reason, she did *not* want to answer it. The hollow, surreal tone of the ringing unnerved her. She stared blankly at the phone for three full rings, then forced herself to pick up the receiver.

"Lisa, you need to drive us to the hospital." Her mother's voice, hysterical. "Right now!"

Lisa heard the dial tone and assumed her mother had hung up to rush back to Dana's side. She wanted to call her back and find out exactly how bad things were, to hear her sister say their mom was overreacting to a stubbed toe, but common sense and raw fear warned her she didn't have time to waste.

Sharon hadn't mentioned where they were, but Lisa knew where to find them. She grabbed her keys and ran to the garage. Her mom spent a few afternoons at Dana's each week, to tidy up the already spotless house and stock the freezer with home cooked meals.

The car whisked the three women down the highway toward the hospital. Dana coughed blood into a green hand towel edged in pink rickrack. Her mother's constant babble was infuriating, but Lisa restrained herself from pushing Sharon out of the moving car.

"It's going to be okay, baby. Keith is on the way and we'll be there in a few minutes. Hurry up, Lisa! Can't you drive any faster? Dana, don't you dare worry about a thing, you're going to be just fine." Sharon droned on and on until they stopped in front of the emergency room doors. Then she bolted from the car and ran into the hospital, screaming at the top of her lungs for Dr. Tolbert and a wheelchair.

"I love Mom, really, I do, but I thought she'd never shut up," Dana said, her voice whispery and labored. She tried to smile, the bloody towel still held beneath her chin.

"Tell me about it." Lisa rolled her eyes and tried to not look terrified. "Here come the orderlies." Unsure what to say at a time like this, she opted for "Love ya, Sis" as two men helped Dana into a wheelchair and pushed her inside the hospital.

Dana waved back, the sopping towel cupped under her face as they wheeled her away.

Keith arrived a few minutes later. They sat and stared at each other while the medical staff treated Dana. Dr. Tolbert had nodded toward them but said nothing before he hurried off to see to his patient.

Fearing this would be the last day of Dana's life, Keith trudged across the waiting room, stuck his face in the corner, and cried into the recesses of the wall. Sharon tried to call her grandchildren but was too flustered to find the send button. Lisa wrestled the cell phone—which wasn't even supposed to be on in their section of the hospital—away from her hysterical mother. She dialed Megan to let her know what was happening and asked her to relay the details to Marcus, in person; the cousins were as close as siblings and Lisa had no doubts that her daughter was the best person to break the news to him. After ordering her to drive safely, she snapped the phone shut.

Better, more optimistic information awaited Marcus and Megan when they arrived at the hospital. Dr. Tolbert explained that Dana was going to pull through. She didn't have a collapsed lung, but a buildup of fluid instead. They gave her medication to slow the hemoptysis, the medical term for coughing up bloody mucus, though it was something she would continue to have to deal with.

They kept Dana overnight as her worried family suffered through a restless evening at the hospital.

ex⌒

Like a blues singer who spent too much time in smoky nightclubs, Dana's voice developed a slight rasp. The medication reduced the bloody sputum, though she continued to cough some up now and then.

Lisa sat with her one particular afternoon, sipping tea as they listened to classical melodies flow through the stereo. She had never understood why Dana liked that kind of music, the type of stuff most people weren't thrilled to hear on elevators rides through upscale buildings. Lisa preferred the local Top 40 station, but had no problem listening to this concerto if it made her sister happy.

"I decided to stop the radiation," Dana said. She took a drink of chamomile tea, sweetened with honey for the soothing effect it had on her sore throat. "Did I tell you that?"

"Uh, no." Lisa felt her forehead pucker into a frown. "Are you sure that's a good idea?"

"It really wasn't doing much good, so I didn't see the point in it." She took another sip of tea. "Goodbye, nuclear sunburn."

"So, what are you going to do next?" Lisa asked. "Do they have some new kind of medicine for you to try or something?"

"Lis, I've decided that I want to live out the time I have left without worrying about side effects and appointments." Dana looked her sister directly in the eyes. "Right now, just think of me as the poster child for that cliché about life being too short."

"You mean . . ." Lisa stopped mid-sentence, her lips pressed together as if someone had glued them shut. Her eyebrow arched as she glared at her sister. "You're just going to give up. You're not even going to try anything else that might help you?"

Dana met her gaze with a face as peaceful as the Dalai Lama's. "I know you love me, but I'm still dying. Not a thing anybody can do about it, not even you."

Lisa wanted to grab Dana by the shoulders and shake some sense into her. How could she sit there, sipping her damn herbal tea, and just decide to die? The last thing she wanted was to start an argument. "Fine," she hissed through gritted teeth, then focused her attention on flipping through one of Keith's hotrod magazines from the coffee table.

"Look, I know you're upset about it," Dana said, "but let me explain this from my point of view." She took a deep breath. "Do you think I enjoyed coffin shopping or the trip to the funeral parlor? Do you think I'm just sitting around here, putting out milk and cookies for the Grim Reaper?"

"No, don't be stupid! I never said-"

"At first, I took care of all the things I needed to get done. It made me feel like I had some small, tiny bit of control over what was happening to me. You have no idea how much I appreciate you going along with me on those trips. Thank you."

Lisa sighed, her anger slipping away. "Please don't thank me. You know you never have to thank me for anything like that."

"I had a lot of time to think about things, especially when I was in the hospital. Like the funeral arrangements, death is something I *do* have to face, like it or not." Dana's voice sounded calm and matter-of-fact, not at all shaky. It was apparent she'd thought out the words she planned to say.

"It's like when Marcus used to drag us to those god-awful haunted houses downtown every October. Remember? They scared the holy crap out of me, but he wanted to go, so I went along."

"Hey, I thought those things were kind of fun." Lisa had always liked to watch the funny faces Dana and the kids made while walking through the spook house.

"Well, you've always been a little warped in the head." Dana paused to grin before she continued. "I'd be right in the middle of it, and I'd want to turn around and run out. But I couldn't leave Marcus standing there, and I think they have some rule about backtracking. Anyway, I had to make myself put one foot in front of the other, ignore the masked people running around with chainsaws and rubber axes the best I could, and get through it. Standing there scared shitless only made things worse."

Lisa got the gist of where Dana was going with this. She felt ashamed of herself for getting mad about something that was not her decision to make.

"That's how we need to get through this, Lis. I'd rather walk out the other side on my own two feet instead of having somebody drag me out, kicking and screaming. It's not something I look forward to, but we're just going to have to take one step at a time, face the demons and the guy with the chainsaw head on, and walk through it."

CHAPTER SIX

Death is beautiful when seen to be a law, and
not an accident - It is as common as life.
~ Henry David Thoreau

Dana hurried outside onto her sister's front
porch when a car pulled into the driveway. A
minute later Lisa walked up the sidewalk,
surprised to find unexpected company waiting
to greet her.

"I have something for you," Dana exclaimed,
feeling her drawn face flush with excitement.
"Now you need be open-minded about it, but
you're gonna love it!"

"What did you do?" Lisa asked, raising an
eyebrow. Dana made her cover her eyes before
allowing her to walk through her own front

door.

"Wait, freeze for just a sec." The sound of scuttling came from the kitchen as Dana let go of her arm. She laughed a few seconds later and announced, "Okay. Surprise! Open your eyes."

"Oh, my God." Speechless, Lisa raised her hand to her cheek. She couldn't help but grin—a very slow, cautious sort of grin, but a grin all the same.

"So? What do you think?" Dana studied Lisa's face, searching for signs of disapproval she hoped she wouldn't find. "Isn't he cute? Don't you just love him already?" She hugged the furry black and tan puppy to emphasize how cuddly he was supposed to be.

"You bought me a . . . grizzly bear?" But Dana could practically see Lisa's heart melt like an ice cube in July as she watched the dog.

"It's a puppy, silly! Megan and Marcus were in on it too, but they left already. Just in case you weren't as thrilled about him as I thought you'd be. We have some brave kids, huh?" Dana said, winking. "Anyway, we got him from this great German shepherd rescue. He's six months old and he's already had basic training and everything."

"He's so *big*." Lisa sat down on the floor beside them and gave the pooch a scritch behind the ear. The oversized pup turned in a circle, smacked them both in the face with his wagging tail, then sat down between his two new playmates. "What's his name?"

"Galahad. I thought we should call him that because he looks so noble and strong, and I knew he'd make you fall in love with his *cute little face. Yes, you will. Lisa loves you already, I can tell*," Dana cooed at the dog in baby talk. "Remember how we used to love reading those stories about King Arthur and the Knights of the Round Table when we were little? Well, say hello to your knight in shining armor."

"Galahad, huh? He'd just better not turn out to be Sir Poops-a-lot."

"Oh, he won't. He's already housebroken. The rescue lady sent a folder full of instructions about when he goes out, how much he eats. Everything you need to know." Dana reached for the red tote bag filled with doggie gear. "His toys are in here, his leash, and here's his brush. He just loves this."

Galahad looked as if he were smiling while Dana brushed him.

"You *do* like him, don't you?" Dana asked, pretty sure her sister did, in fact, want to keep the gigantic puppy lying between them. She breathed a little easier after Lisa thanked her and kissed Galahad on his fuzzy head.

Dana was happy she could do something like this for her. Lisa wasn't much of a people person, so Dana worried about what would happen when she was no longer around to keep her company. Then, like magic, a puppy had popped into her mind. They'd both wanted one so badly when they were children, but their mother wouldn't allow it.

The puppy would be perfect for Lisa, especially later on, when Dana knew her sister would have trouble coping. She couldn't just lay in bed all day, alone and depressed, not if she had a dog to take care of. Nope, Lisa would have to get up to feed and walk Galahad. He needed to go out a few times every day, and Lisa would have no choice but to take him.

Her main reason for giving Galahad to Lisa, however, was for companionship. Watching her now, nuzzling up to the puppy like a five-year-old to a giant teddy bear, Dana knew she'd made a wise decision. This was one gift sure to keep on giving, long after Dana passed away.

Like so many rescued animals proved to be, Galahad was a quick learner and eager to please, and he'd been his foster mom's star pupil. He walked nicely on the leash and practically dove into a 'down' when asked. If put on a 'stay' command, the dog wouldn't move a millimeter from his spot while Lisa walked around him, left the room, or even danced a little jig, shaking her behind as Galahad tilted his head quizzically to the side. For parlor tricks, he could fetch, roll over, shake hands, and even pull off a pretty decent high five.

Galahad seemed to sense something special about Dana, though it was impossible for him to understand her terminal illness, and kept her in his field of vision whenever she was around. If she got tired and sat down abruptly—something she was prone to do quite often now, as she grew weaker—Galahad trotted over and plopped down beside her.

His big brown eyes never held pity during Dana's visits, only love and a willingness to please. If she had the strength to throw his tennis ball, he'd fetch it as often as she wanted, his massive tail wagging the whole time. He couldn't lecture her for overdoing it, unlike the people who loved her.

May turned to June while Dana's health continued to roller skate downhill. Her whole family seemed to be stuck in eggshell mode, but she counted on Big Sis to give her some normalcy and the occasional good-natured argument. Still, she realized Lisa handled her with kid gloves, as if she would crumble to pieces in front of her eyes at any given moment.

Dana's logical mind knew her mother and husband did things they thought were in her best interest, but she resented being treated like a helpless toddler. Her family obviously loved her, but did they have to act so damn stupid? When Sharon tried to spoon feed her chicken soup, Dana snapped. "Mom, I have lung cancer, not two broken arms and a cold, for God's sake."

The way Keith suffered broke Dana's heart.

He tried to put up a strong front for her benefit, but she knew what he did at night after he thought she'd fallen asleep. He would stare at her for minutes on end, as if watching her breathe would prevent her from ever stopping. After a while he'd turn over to face the wall, and cry into his pillow. She felt his sobs in the bed's subtle tremors.

CHAPTER SEVEN

Death must be so beautiful.
To lie in the soft brown earth, with the grasses
waving above one's head, and listen to silence.
~ Oscar Wilde

Fate refused to let Dana forget she lived on borrowed time. The night of June 13th brought another hospital trip, after Dana had poked Keith awake because she was having a great deal of trouble breathing.

Her family waited, wondering whether she'd live to see the sunrise in the morning, while Dr. Tolbert 'worked on' Dana. In the trench coat she'd thrown on over her nightgown before bolting out the front door, Lisa visualized white-clad mechanics 'working on' her sister, hoping against everything they'd wield their magic wrenches to keep Dana's engine running a little while longer.

"I'll wait until we know something before I call Marcus," Keith said as he patted his mother-in-law on the knee. Lisa wished Sharon would be still instead of worrying herself to pieces between them.

The trio sprang to their feet when Dr. Tolbert entered the room.

Lisa caught the hint of a comforting smile on his face and knew her sister was still alive. She ran her hand through her tousled brown hair as a hundred pounds of worry drained through her shoes and into the floor.

"Dana suffered a bronchial blockage," Dr. Tolbert explained, "a common problem for lung cancer patients. She's going to pull through. We'll keep her overnight but she should be able to go home tomorrow afternoon, so long as her condition remains stable."

❧

Dana recuperated at home for the next couple of weeks. Sharon and Lisa took turns staying with her during the day while Keith was at work. Plagued by coughing fits, Dana took pills for the ever-growing pain in her chest.

Even with her mother stepping ever so slightly on Dana's nerves, she appreciated all the love and support from her family. She did *not* like to be babied, however, and wanted a chance to do the things she was still able to do. Staying cooped up in her home in July was getting to her. She yearned to go out and enjoy the sunshine, terminal illness be damned. While Keith and Sharon would have loved to keep her locked in a hermetically sealed bubble, she counted on Big Sis to help her. She knew Lisa had tried to fight her eggshell urges ever since the day Dana told her she'd decided to stop treatment. Although she would have liked to set Dana on a pile of feather pillows in some safe medical environment, Lisa did her best to make her sister's life easier.

A memory Dana hadn't thought of in years came to mind. When she was six, the class bully had yanked her Hello Kitty lunchbox out of her hands, pushed her down, and ate her Twinkie while she ran to hide in the restroom. That afternoon, with her skinned knees and puffy red face, she'd ran home, straight into Big Sis's arms. The next day, the little Twinkie thief sported a black eye and Lisa got a week of detention, but no one ever bullied Dana again.

If only Lisa could kick cancer's ass as easily as she'd taken on that bully. Too bad that wasn't possible.

Dana seldom asked for favors, but one afternoon, after their mother left for the day, she called Lisa and positively begged to go out somewhere, anywhere with fresh air and sunshine. Lisa agreed. The summer humidity made it much harder for Dana to breathe, so they planned to go early, before it got too hot.

The eighty-four-degree weather felt heavenly compared to the humid hundred-degree scorchers of the previous week. A gentle breeze carried the scent of honeysuckle from mounds that grew over the park fence. The garden spot by the entrance called to mind scenes from Shakespeare's *A Midsummer's*

Night Dream; the hummingbirds and butterflies that hovered near the hyssop and roses in the early morning sunlight could, if seen at just the right angle, easily be mistaken for fairies.

Near a cluster of oak trees, they spread an old blanket on the ground. Dana kicked off her sandals and lay down on her back to let the sunshine warm her face and toes. That lasted for all of thirty seconds before Galahad, wanting to regain the attention lavished all over him during the car ride, licked her on the nose.

"This pup needs some exercise, Lis," Dana said. "Pass me that tote bag." She fished out a red Frisbee, tennis ball, and a ridiculously long leash, which she snapped onto Galahad's collar in place of the shorter lead. "Okay, big boy. Go get it," Dana exclaimed, throwing the tennis ball out onto the lush green dandelion-studded lawn. They watched like proud parents as Galahad ran to fetch it. Dana was able to remain seated while she held the leash; the thing was so long, the German shepherd only reached the end of it once, when the ball had gone on a downhill roll.

They watched a flock of mallards make a graceful landing on the water. Ripples radiated around the ducks as they paddled across the surface.

"You want to go for a walk around the lake?"

"I don't know." Lisa chewed her lip for a few seconds. "That's a pretty long walk. You sure it's a good idea?" She worried that Dana, so pale and weak, would bring on a coughing fit or something much worse if she overexerted herself. Keith hadn't been very keen on the outing, and if she made Dana sicker, she was afraid they might not have a chance to go out together like this again.

"Oh. I get it. Afraid you'll tire yourself out, huh?" Dana smiled and put her shoes back on. "Why don't we compromise, then. Those pine trees are just, oh, about a fourth of the way, so you could probably make it there and back. You're not that old and decrepit. Yet."

"Old and decrepit!"

"Don't worry. Me and Galahad can help you, if your old legs give out." Dana got up and started walking, Galahad by her side.

Lisa joined them, feeling good about having brought her back to a place they'd enjoyed so much when they were little girls. With each step, she prayed the walk wouldn't be too hard on her ailing sister.

Adrenaline must have helped Dana make her way to the thicket of pine trees that grew by the water's edge and reflected on the surface like an enchanted underwater kingdom.

The pace was much slower on their return trip. Dana was short of breath and coughing a bit, so they stopped to sit on a large rock near the halfway point. Her spirits stayed high, however, and she didn't let her frailty spoil the day. Lisa tried to act as if she didn't notice, and filled the break with juicy gossip she'd picked up in town. Galahad stopped to chase orange and black Monarch butterflies on the way back to the car, which gave them another excuse to rest and watch his antics.

Lisa put the blanket in the trunk as thoughts of gratitude whirled through her mind. When a person truly understands life's brevity, the small things stand out in vivid clarity. The sun shines brighter, grass is greener, and flowers smell sweeter. A dog's wagging tail melts a person's heart like an ice cream cone by a campfire, and a summer day with her sister becomes pure Nirvana.

CHAPTER EIGHT

Life and death are balanced
on the edge of a razor.
~ Homer

On a sunny August afternoon, Lisa and Dana watched a chick flick on HBO. "Is the herbal tea helping your throat?" Lisa refilled her sister's cup, stirred in the honey until it dissolved, then passed it to her.

"Thanks." Dana sipped the warm brew. "It feels soothing on the way down."

Dana had felt pretty bad for the past couple days. Her voice became scratchier as her cough grew more persistent. Red washcloths camouflaged the bloody mucus her lungs expelled.

The coughing increased over a span of about fifteen minutes. Then Dana reached across the couch to grab Lisa's arm.

"Can't breathe." Dana clutched at the neckline of her shirt. "Chest pains . . . and my shoulder." A vein bulged in her neck.

Lisa took a deep breath and willed herself not to panic when she saw that Dana's skin had turned grayish-blue. She didn't want to scare Dana even more by letting her know how terrified she was.

"I'll get the keys. Don't worry, we can be at the hospital in a jiff." She grabbed for her purse, but Dana's hand tightened around her wrist.

"No time . . . ambulance." She had a hard time drawing in enough air to speak.

Within minutes of the 911 call, EMTs invaded the living room. Dana was en route to the hospital shortly thereafter. Lisa rode along, seated behind the gurney. She couldn't reach Dana's hand, so she stroked her hair instead, so she'd know Big Sis was right there beside her. Lights flashed, sirens screamed, and she watched in horror as medics plunged a plastic tube into Dana's chest, which caused a sickening sputter of air to spew into the ambulance.

Lisa called the rest of the family after they whisked Dana into the hospital. She'd been shocked at the speed in which an ordinary afternoon turned into a medical emergency. Making up for lost time, she dialed Keith first, then her mother and Megan. Keith would pick up Marcus on his way to the hospital, a relief to Lisa since she had no idea how to explain the situation to her nephew. All she could tell her family when they asked her what happened was that Dana had chest pains and couldn't breathe. She had no idea whether she'd come down with pneumonia, was having a heart attack, or, God forbid, the cancer was about to claim her life.

In dreamlike succession, her family arrived at the ER.

Dr. Tolbert ushered them into a consultation room, his stoic expression unreadable. Keith, Sharon, and Marcus took seats opposite the oncologist while Lisa and Megan stood directly behind them, holding each other's hands as they listened.

Dr. Tolbert spoke, his backbone ramrod straight as he peered at them through his bifocals, his voice knowledgeable yet compassionate. "Dana's in intensive care and we're treating her for pneumothorax."

Keith absentmindedly rubbed the underside of his wedding ring with his thumb. "Excuse me, but for what? Neuroforax?"

"Pneumothorax. I'm sorry, I should have explained it better," Dr. Tolbert replied. "That's the hard way of saying her lungs collapsed. There was a buildup of air between her lungs and the wall of her chest cavity, obviously due to complications from the cancer. The EMTs administered a tube to get the extra air off her chest on their way here. As far as I can tell, I don't believe she sustained any brain damage. It's a good thing she got here in time."

Keith, Lisa, and the rest of the family continued to stare at the doctor, unsure whether to be thrilled about the no brain damage part or mortified by the collapsed lung explanation.

"Okay," Keith said, attempting to pull his thoughts together into something coherent.

"Exactly how is she? Can we see her?"

"Dana is in critical condition right now, Mr. Yager. One of her lungs has been re-inflated and they're treating the other one as we speak. We're going to need to leave the chest tube in over the next day or so, in case the lung collapses again. We don't know yet whether there was any damage to her cardiovascular system. If all goes well, we can run tests on that tomorrow."

"So when can Mom come home?" A pale complexion and red-rimmed eyes showed Marcus's anxiety. "She *is* gonna be alright, isn't she?" The last was more of a plea than a question. He glanced down when his grandmother's hand covered his own.

Dr. Tolbert's eyes shifted to the wall across the room as he spoke. "We can't say right now. She's in critical condition, she'll have to remain in the ICU unit until she improves, but we should be able to stabilize her lungs." He looked back at Marcus apologetically. "I wish I knew more to tell you."

The family took turns sitting with Dana. Hospital rules dictated that only two visitors could be in each of the Intensive Care Units at any given time. The five of them rotated every hour. Those not in the ICU waited in the lounge and stared at the small television mounted in the corner, flipped through magazines from the rack on the wall, made small talk with one another, or just gazed into space as worry overtook their minds. They tried to sleep on the waiting room couch and ate cafeteria food. Two days of this routine turned them into emotionally frazzled zombies.

Dana's lungs started functioning but an infection developed. Antibiotics fought to keep the fever under control. Painkillers flowed through her IV drip to keep her unconscious most of the time and woozy when awake. Lying there in a near comatose condition, she coughed up blood-tinged mucus that her loved ones wiped away, careful not to disturb any of the wires that trailed from Dana to the monitors beeping beside her bed.

On the second night in Intensive Care, Dana's fever shot back up and she began wheezing. Lisa sat alone in the room on the edge of her sister's bed, holding her hand, talking to her even though she was unconscious. Afraid her sister would stop breathing at any moment, she broke down.

Lisa cried in great heaving sobs, glad no one else was in the room to see her lose her composure.

Why the hell was this happening to Dana? She was the last person in the world who deserved to go out like this, hooked up to machines, gasping for air. Lisa would gladly have traded places with her, were it in her power to do so.

Her mind flashed back to a conversation they'd had a few months earlier. She cried harder remembering all the things her sister had said she'd never be able to do. No grandkids, no trips to Europe, no hot air balloon rides, no more holidays.

No more life, Lisa added, crying into the blanket, her head next to Dana's side. She longed to hug her so badly, but was afraid any extra pressure, no matter how slight, might make Dana stop those awful rattling sounds that passed for breathing.

She knew Dana just wanted to live as full a

life as she was able. Guilt washed over Lisa for her own overprotective tendencies since the diagnosis, especially the time she'd gotten mad at Dana when she'd stopped taking treatments. Now she understood why Dana made that decision—to avoid even more time spent suffering the way she was right now.

"I'm so sorry, Dana," Lisa sobbed, her strained voice soft beside her sister's ear. "If I could go back and do it over, I'd do things so differently. I'd tell Mom to lay off. God knows she means well, but she was about to drive you crazy. I'd take you out on the town when you felt like it, instead of insisting we stay in watching DVDs, and we'd go outside in the sunshine anytime you want."

Lisa blew her nose on a tissue. "I'd even bring you wine, like you asked for last week. I'm so sorry I didn't. I was afraid it wouldn't be a good idea for you to mix booze with your painkillers, but hell, I don't guess anything could be worse than this, huh?" Tears raced down Lisa's face and dripped off her chin, onto the tidy white blanket tucked around Dana. "And I'd let you walk anywhere you damn well wanted to in the park. I'd just carry you out piggyback when you couldn't go any farther."

Dana coughed in violent spasms. Lisa grabbed one of the washcloths stacked on the tray and wiped away sputum as panic set in.

"I love you so much, Dana. I don't know if you can hear me, but if you can, I want you to know how important you are to me. You're my best friend. I don't know what I'd have done through the years, during those hard times in my life, without you there beside me. . . . but I don't want you to worry about anything. I promise to look after Marcus and-"

A red light on one of the monitors interrupted, flashing and beeping a signal of alarm. Footsteps hurried toward the room.

"Oh my God." She spoke quickly, to say what she had to before the stampede of nurses burst in. "I love you Dana . . . . Goodbye."

Confused and helpless, Lisa stood frozen beside the bed. A matronly nurse put her arm around her and led her from the room so the medical staff could attend to Dana. Without thinking about what she did, Lisa hugged the RN, buried her face on her shoulder, and wailed.

When Lisa eventually calmed down and pulled away, she made her way toward her waiting family.

She trudged slowly down the hall, wishing she had more time left to spend with her sister. Even just one more day.

CHAPTER NINE

As a well-spent day brings happy sleep,
so a life well used brings happy death.
~ Leonardo da Vinci

A small miracle occurred and Dana pulled through. She waved good-bye to the nurses a few days later, eager to leave the chest tube behind and return to the comforts of home.

Her family was thankful to see her escape the hospital alive. Emotionally drained, they didn't quite know what to do with themselves.

The night after Dana's release, Lisa snuggled into her own bed, a nice change after so many sleepless nights on the lumpy couch at the hospital. Unfortunately, a nightmare interrupted her peaceful snooze.

In the dream, she saw Dana laid out in a coffin in the funeral parlor. No mourners occupied the empty seats, just two nurses on the back row filling out medical charts. Lisa walked toward the casket and noticed that Dana appeared as she had at the age of eight. She wore the navy suit they'd bought at the mall, but now it hung off her transformed pre-teen body. The mortician had smeared orange blush on Dana's cheeks, which made her look as if she died during a game of dress up. An enormous spray of black lilies draped over the open coffin lid above her face.

She gazed down into the casket and saw something in the crook of Dana's arm. It was the pink teddy bear they'd shared as children. The last Lisa had seen of the toy was the day she and Dana, both under eleven years old at the time, had gotten into a huge fight over who got to hold her during their tea party. A tugging match ensued, which left Miss Tinkie's cloth body ripped in half as a flurry of stuffing flew around their bedroom.

Magically repaired in dreamland, Miss Tinkie had found her way into Dana's lifeless arms. Lisa looked from the toy back to her sister's face. Dana's skin had turned gray, making the garish rouge on her cheeks stand out even more. Tufts of snow filled the casket, and frost shimmered on her eyelids.

The leash Lisa suddenly found in her hand pulled taut as Galahad tried to drag her away from the coffin. She turned, shocked to see the room now brimmed with spectral mourners dressed in black hooded cloaks. Ungodly wailing filled the funeral home until Lisa put her hands over her ears to block out the cacophony.

A toothless old man with a shovel leered at her when Galahad led her from the room. She paused to look back, needing one last glimpse at her sister's face.

Grim reapers surrounded the coffin, all trying to close the lid and nail the casket shut. Dana's arms stuck out the side as she shrieked, "Don't let them put me in the ground. Help me!"

Galahad jumped onto the bed when Lisa woke up screaming, drenched in sweat. She hugged his neck, glad he was there to comfort her. When she finally managed to fall back to sleep, it was with one arm draped over the huge puppy lying beside her. From that point on, the German shepherd had a new bed.

❧

The dream haunted Lisa the next morning. She poured kibble into Galahad's bowl and sat down at the kitchen table with a steaming cup of coffee. To rid her mind of the lingering images from last night's morbid nightmare, she focused on her plans for the day. It was her turn to stay with Dana.

Her mind snapped back to the Intensive Care Unit when Dana had nearly died. Lisa remembered apologizing for being so overprotective, and recalled things she wanted to go back and change.

An epiphany struck her in the middle of her forehead with such force, she could almost feel a light bulb pulsate in the air above her skull.

"Dana is still *alive*." Lisa exhaled as she realized the true gift fate had granted them both. "And she needs to *live*."

How many hours on how many days had Lisa

spent crying, petrified because her sister was dying? Too many to count. Some of the tears were for her impending death, true, but Lisa realized now that most were over how much she would miss Dana, selfish tears robbing them both of precious time that should be better spent.

Torn between kicking herself in the head and jumping for joy, Lisa promised herself things would be different from now on.

Never again would she mourn someone whose heart still beat, someone able to talk, to laugh, to feel joy. There would be plenty of time for goodbyes and boo-hooing at Dana's funeral. Why should Dana have to waste the precious few moments she had left watching her family grieve? That just didn't seem like a fair deal. A terminal disease was bad enough; her sister needn't be subjected to everyone else's depression and fear at a time like this.

A new motto filled her mind, a mantra she would chant over and over to herself in the following weeks, when times threatened to turn dark: *No more tears for the living.*

❧

"Morning, sleepy head." Lisa nudged Dana awake on the couch. "Time to get up and get dressed."

"What?" Dana sat up and rubbed her eyes. She'd fallen back to sleep after Keith left for work, and now she yawned at the smiling face that greeted her. "I think somebody must've ODed on coffee."

"I did enjoy my java this morning, come to think of it." Lisa grinned down at her. "What do you want to wear?"

Dana peered at her through the corner of her eye. "Well, a Vera Wang gown would be just lovely. Maybe one with sequins to match the couch I'll be propped up on all day." The edges of her mouth turned up slightly as curiosity settled on her face.

"Let me see what I can find in your closet." Lisa reentered the room a minute later. "Couldn't find your Vera Wang, but this T-shirt and pair of jeans ought to do." She tossed the clothes onto Dana's lap. "You need any help?"

The chest tube incision was still tender when she raised her arms, so she let Lisa help slip the t-shirt over her head. Lisa threaded a belt through the jean loops before handing them to her. Dana grew thinner by the day, as evidenced by the loose, baggy fit of her pants. She slid her feet into her favorite flip-flops and asked the obvious question. "Where are we going?"

"Nowhere special. I have to run some errands so I thought you could ride along. Figured you might want to get out of the house for a while." She knew her sister was still frail, too weak yet even to sit through a movie at the theatre. However, she also knew Dana loved riding shotgun with the windows down, and that she'd be happy to sit in the car while Lisa ran into the bank and dropped some books off at the library. "Anywhere you'd like to go while we're out?"

"I really don't feel like going *in* anywhere," Dana said, obviously pleased with the upgrade in the day's schedule. "But yeah, going to town again sounds like a nice idea. Bring me my red baseball cap and a brush and I'll be ready in a jiff." She pulled her hair into a ponytail through the back of her cap and dabbed on some lip balm. Never one to go out looking her worst, sporty chic was a great alternative.

The previous night's rain cooled things down to a comfortable temperature, warm but not too humid. Dana seemed to enjoy the fresh breeze that caressed her cheek through the open window.

Lisa hopped out at the bank and left Dana fiddling with the knobs on the car stereo as she plugged her MP3 player into it. She returned to the driver's seat to find Dana swaying to classical music, eyes closed as sunbeams played across her face.

"I thought I'd accidentally stepped into an elevator." Lisa grimaced as she fastened her seatbelt. "What the hell are we listening to?"

"Tchaikovsky, from Swan Lake. Isn't it cool?"

"Sure, if you're a hundred and two." She hated this kind of crappy music more than words could express, but since Dana liked it so much, Lisa was happy to compromise. "Tell you what, we'll take turns."

"Okay." Dana flashed a mischievous grin. "My turn first."

"Fine. Every fifteen minutes, we'll swap control of the stereo. You listen to this snappy shit from the seventeenth century-"

"It was composed," Dana interrupted, ever the stickler for details, "in the 1876, actually."

"Well, no matter how old it is," Lisa said, pausing to smirk at her sister, "you listen to it for the next fifteen minutes, then I'll put in my Lady Gaga CD. Fair enough?"

"Sounds fair to me." Dana cranked up the volume, waved her pointed fingers like conductor's batons, and bobbed her head in time to the music.

A couple of teenage boys walking down the sidewalk found her antics hysterically funny. One shouted "Rock on" when the car passed by.

Their next stop was the public library, the same beautiful old building where they'd spent so much spare time when they were little girls. In their eyes, the converted Victorian mansion would always seem like a castle haunted by characters from their favorite books. They both still loved the antique smell of varnished woodwork and musty pages, the texture of weathered covers under their fingertips, and the way a good story could sweep them away from their real lives and into daydreams of romance and adventure.

"I'll only be a minute. Just need to drop these in the box." Lisa, an avid reader, leaned into the backseat for a pile of books. The stack consisted of two romances, one true crime mystery, and a thick hardback horror novel about a band of vampires running amuck in Tennessee.

"Oh, here. Let me." Dana reached to take the books.

The drop box in front of the library was just a short stone's throw away, though she would have to climb up a few stairs to get to it.

"Don't-" Lisa bit her lips to shut herself up. No more eggshells. That's what she'd promised, that she'd let her do whatever the hell she wanted. Lisa didn't like the idea of Dana carrying a bunch of books up the steps, but in the grand scheme of things, it really wasn't such a big deal. To cover what she'd almost said, she continued, ". . . don't drop 'em." She forced a smile and passed her the books.

Pure gratitude shone through Dana's eyes. "Don't worry. I won't." There was no need for more words. They both understood completely.

Her feet moved at a slow pace, her hand running along the railing, but Dana made the short walk with no problems. Back in her seat a little later, she suggested, "Maybe we can catch a movie next week, if I'm feeling up to it."

"Sounds good to me."

Lisa didn't bother to change the classical music blaring through her speakers, even though it was her turn.

❦

"Hi, come on in." Keith opened the door when Lisa arrived that weekend to take Dana to the Bluebird Cinema. He leaned in to whisper, "She thinks this will make things easier on you later on, so you can associate the damn outfit with happy times. Probably not something a psychiatrist would approve of, but it made sense to Dana. Try not to freak out."

Lisa had no idea what he was talking about, until he stepped aside to let her in. Eyebrow raised as she steadied herself against the doorframe, she desperately tried to see the humor in the situation. "A bit overdressed, aren't we?"

"Nope, I want to get my money's worth out of this outfit. Makes my butt look cute, doesn't it?" Dana turned and shook her behind. Then, runway style, she pivoted around, a playful grin on her lips as she modeled the navy suit she'd bought to be buried in. Alterations compensated for the large amount of weight she'd lost in the three months since she'd picked it out.

"You're beautiful, butt and all." Lisa needed a reason to avert her eyes before she broke into tears, so she glanced at her watch. "We'd better get moving or we'll be late for the movie."

Dana walked out first, which gave Lisa an opportunity to roll her eyes at Keith after she wiped away the damned tear that seemed intent on streaking her mascara. She felt a sympathetic pat on her back as she moved past him.

Keith called after them, his voice masked with happiness, "Have a good time."

They drove through a liquor store after the show, a bawdy comedy about a runaway nun on a gambling steak in Vegas, and picked up a bottle of Chardonnay. Back at Dana's house, they stopped at one glass each. Neither verbalized the fact that it wasn't a good idea to combine too much alcohol with the medication.

Dana hugged her at the door on her way out. "Thanks so much for everything, Lis. It feels almost like old times. Love you."

Lisa turned quickly to walk down the sidewalk, glad the darkness hid her face. "Love you, too."

Dana was alive and well right now, and that's what she needed to focus on. In her head, she chanted, *No more tears for the living.*

CHAPTER TEN

Theirs not to make reply,
Theirs not to reason why,
Theirs but to do and die.
~ Alfred Lord Tennyson

"Night, Marcus. Love you too," Dana said before she disconnected and set her cell down beside her on the porch swing. Marcus called every evening, just to say goodnight and talk with her a few minutes.

When fall classes started a few weeks ago, he almost hadn't gone back. He thought he should take the semester off to stay home and take care of her, but the last thing Dana wanted was to have her son waste his time, worried sick as he watched her grow weaker by the day. So now, after a little strong-arming from his parents, Marcus stayed in his college dorm room during the week but made the forty-five minute drive home each weekend, a compromise he insisted on.

She cherished every moment with Marcus, her sweet, sweet boy who gave up frat parties to play board games with his mom when she felt up to it, and sat listening to classical music with her when that was all she had the energy to do. She loved him so much, and hated that she'd have leave him without a mother. Lisa's promise to always be there for him was the only thing that quelled Dana's maternal anxiety. Even in death, she knew she would miss him, an eternal ache to keep her child, no matter his age, safe in her arms forever.

But that was something she had no control over, and it was best not to dwell on sadness. Instead, she closed her eyes and pictured Marcus's smile as she replayed their conversation in her head, thankful for every moment she had left to spend with him and all the people she loved. So grateful for each day in her short future.

A gentle drizzle raised a light fog over the street in front of her house, the wet asphalt still hot from the August sun that had sat a few hours before. Keith was asleep in bed, thanks to his prescription sleeping pills, so Dana had slipped outside to enjoy the night air. This had become her favorite nightly ritual, the only time she spent in solitude, away from the watchful worried eyes of her family. She loved to listen to the crickets chirp and gaze at the stars, her mind free of troubled thoughts as moonlight glistened off the dewy grass.

She inhaled the clean, misty scent of rain and relaxed into the comfort of her porch swing, glad the moisture hadn't soaked into the cushions. She enjoyed this type of weather, when mother nature showered the earth and left the world daisy fresh and replenished. Raindrops tapped a soft cadence against the oak leaves on the branches that sheltered her home, then turned to staccato drip-drops as they hit the roof. Nature's symphony.

A car drove by, its wheels fanning puddle water up over the sidewalk in a graceful arch. Dana leaned forward and extended her arm past the porch rail to let a few cool raindrops dot the palm of her hand. She was tempted to sleep out there, curled up on the swing, but she knew she had to go in to bed soon. That was okay, since she planned to open the window just enough to let the scent and sounds of the rain help her drift off into a peaceful sleep. Nothing made her feel more comfortable than snuggling up, warm and dry and safe, while gentle rain rejuvenated everything around her.

CHAPTER ELEVEN

When you were born, you cried
and the world rejoiced.
Live your life so that when you die,
the world cries and you rejoice.
~ Cherokee Wisdom

"How long till we get there?" Dana asked. Headlights cut a path through the darkness while Lisa drove down a gravel road in the wee hours of the morning. "Can't you at least give me a hint?"

The day before, Lisa had called to tell Dana she had a little something planned. Early. In fact, Lisa told her, she'd be coming to pick her up at three o'clock the next morning. "Be ready when I get there, 'cause you're not going to want to miss this. And bring a camera with lots of film." That was all Dana got out of her before she'd said, "See ya bright and early," and hung up.

A Mona Lisa smirk tugged at Lisa's lips. "We're almost there. And nope, I'm not giving you any hints. Don't get your panties in a bunch, you'll find out soon enough." They'd been on the road for about two hours now. With Dana squinting into the darkness, her face aglow with excitement, Lisa couldn't resist teasing her. "Boy, are you gonna love this. Sure am glad *I* know what's happening."

"You're so mean!" Dana bounced a crumpled napkin off her sister's head. Both laughed until a field full of headlights and people moving equipment around came into view. "Hey, what's going on over there?"

"Hmmmm. Don't know." Lisa applied the brakes and hit her turn signal, even though no one was on the country road behind her at this hour.

Dana peered at the activity buzzing a few feet from the car. A colossal wicker basket lay on its side with a flame shooting out toward a huge pile of material. She gasped, her brown eyes wide and twinkling. "Oh, sweet Jesus! Is that a hot air balloon?"

"Could be." Lisa snapped a picture of Dana with her mouth hanging open.

This was the only thing from Dana's stuff-she'd-never-be-able-to-do list Lisa could actually make happen. Grandchildren and a trip to Europe were out of the question now, but a balloon ride seemed well worth the five hundred bucks it cost to give her this last big adventure.

Perched on the tailgate of one of the trucks, they watched the crew inflate the humongous balloon with hot air. Passengers were welcome to help with the inflation and deflation process, but when Lisa called to schedule the flight, she'd asked them not to mention that. Standing during the ride would be physically taxing enough in Dana's condition.

The yellow orb grew bigger, until it revealed a giant hummingbird logo under 'Beaumont' in red lettering. In just twenty minutes, the balloon swelled to its full size.

Dawn barely glowed in the distance when

pilot Lance Beaumont introduced himself. After the mandatory safety lecture, they signed a risk waiver and climbed aboard.

"There's a stool," Lance pointed out, "in case anybody wants to sit down."

"Oh, I'm gonna stand up for this." Dana looked like a kid in a candy store. "I've wanted to ride in one of these ever since I saw *Around the World in Eighty Days* when I was little. Lisa, th-"

Lisa cut her off, an index finger raised in warning. "Don't even think about saying the t-word again." The fifth time Dana had thanked her while they watched the balloon inflate, Lisa promised to throw her overboard if she said 'thanks' one more time. "This is just a little something I wanted us to do together."

"I was only saying" Dana said, feigning wide-eyed innocence, "this is gonna be great."

Lance released the ropes that anchored them to the ground when they reached an elevation of five hundred feet. In front of their eyes, the sunrise painted the sky pink with nature's watercolors. They could see for miles, over tree-studded hills and lush green fields of corn and soybeans. Birds flew by at eye level, glancing at the odd creatures in the balloon before they continued on their way.

"Oh, look over there!" Dana pointed to a patch of wild flowers below them. "It's just like a Monet painting, but even prettier."

The balloon's basket felt stable under their feet. They could hardly detect any movement at all, except when the wind changed course and sent them in another direction.

They snapped pictures of the scenery while Lance doled out trivial information about the balloon. "It takes fifteen gallons of propane to fuel this baby for a one-hour flight. We're traveling at about ten knots, or eleven miles per hour, and on a clear day, you can see things in a fifty-mile radius. That's why the North and South both used balloons during the Civil War for reconnaissance, so the soldiers could find out what the enemy was up to."

"I didn't even know these things existed back then." Lisa clicked a shot of the pink-glazed horizon.

"I can't imagine anything more beautiful than this," Dana said. "It's so peaceful." The serene expression on her face belied the fact she had trouble standing.

Lisa noticed a tremor in Dana's left arm, the one she leaned on with her hand wrapped around the lip of the basket. She wouldn't spoil things by telling her to sit down. Though sick and weakened, Dana seemed to be having the time of her life. Something was different about the way she held herself, up there in the clouds. An emotion Lisa couldn't quite read glowed on her face.

In one swift movement, Lisa scooped Dana's arm around her own neck and put her right arm around her waist, supporting most of Dana's tiny frame. Dana smiled in gratitude, then both gazed back at the spellbinding view.

Later, when it was time to set the balloon down, Lance said, "Ladies, I don't think we could find a better spot to land if we tried." He'd explained earlier that since there was no way to steer a balloon, they'd go wherever the wind carried them in an hour. They descended on the edge of a sunflower field, the orange and gold blossoms growing larger and more detailed as they approached. Lisa snapped a few more pictures, imagining this must be how it felt to be a giant bee, buzzing around in search of nectar, or pollen, or whatever it was that bees snacked on.

The basket touched down, bunny hopping twice over the tall green stalks before it came to a complete stop. The chase crew's van pulled off the road near the balloon. Mr. Beaumont helped them climb out into the shoulder-high flowers.

"Let's just hope the farmer who owns this field doesn't pass by for a few minutes," he joked and gave them a wink. "If I was you, I think I might be tempted to swipe a bouquet while this baby deflates."

"Good idea," Dana agreed, "We just might do that." She and Lisa picked two colossal bouquets while the crew got back to work. They dampened napkins with bottled water and wrapped them around the stems, to keep the flowers from wilting on the long ride home.

Seated on the ground at the edge of the field, they watched the crew let the air out of the balloon. Then out of the van came a small table with an ice bucket and a bottle of bubbly. Flute glasses were set up on one end, a tray of cheese and fruit beside that, and a bowl of dark chocolate candies shaped like stars.

Lance popped the cork for the traditional end-of-ride celebration. Everyone clapped and cheered as he filled glasses and passed them around. "Which one of you little ladies wants to honor us with a toast?"

"I will." Dana stepped up and raised her glass, its bubbling contents reflecting the morning sun like molten gold. She closed one eye and searched for the right words. "Here's to living in the moment."

Glasses clinked all around.

Lisa took a few hearty gulps of champagne to help fight back the salt water burning her tear ducts. *No more tears for the living*, she reminded herself. *Dana's alive, here and now, enjoying the hell out of this day, and that's all that matters.*

The chase crew made a circle around the passengers, then Lance stepped flamboyantly into the middle. "Attention everybody. On behalf of Beaumont Balloons, I'd like to present these two brave ladies with commemorative flight certificates and these pretty little pins. Lisa Elkins." He bestowed the perks on his first passenger, then read the next name off the parchment. "Dana Yager."

Dana beamed when Lance fastened the dainty hummingbird pin to her shirt. "Did you enjoy yourself, honey?" His eyes crinkled above his smile as he handed her the certificate.

She answered him with a hug. "It's a memory I'll carry in my heart forever."

The balloon flight touched her more than anyone could imagine.

CHAPTER TWELVE

The fear of death follows from the fear of life.
A man who lives fully is prepared to die
at any time.
~ Mark Twain

September 20th,
Mercy United Hospital, 5:13 p.m.

Sharon shuffled through the waiting room door on the cancer wing. Tears streamed from her bloodshot eyes. She stopped behind Lisa's chair and rested a hand on her shoulder, a wad of Kleenex wedged between her palm and her daughter's blouse. "You can go in now."

Lisa couldn't bear to look at her mother's face. If she did, she knew she would break down and cry like a two-year-old, the very last thing anyone here needed to see. She patted the hand on her shoulder, then stood and turned toward the door.

She took a deep breath as she approached Dana's hospital bed, then sat on the edge beside her. At least the cancer wing felt a bit cozier than the Intensive Care Unit, which overflowed with equipment and the sterile smell of alcohol. This room had light blue blankets on the bed, upholstered armchairs that reclined into something a person could actually fall asleep in, and colorful abstract paintings positioned on the wall where the patient could appreciate them. An IV drip and a large monitor stood to one side of the headboard. This type of room served two purposes: a room for recovering from cancer-related problems; and the reason Dana occupied it now—a serene, comfortable place in which to die.

Three nights ago, Dana had awakened with terrible chest pains, the worst she'd ever complained of. Sputum spewed from her coughing lungs like lava from the heart of a volcano. Her laborious breathing made speech next to impossible, and she seemed unable to draw in enough air to fuel her vocal chords. Tests reported what everyone expected and feared. The cancer had metastasized even more. It spread farther through her disease-ravaged body and invaded all the organs and soft tissue it touched.

In the consultation room, Dr. Tolbert spoke the words the family had dreaded since the diagnosis in April, just five short months before. "Dana's organs are shutting down. We're giving her morphine for the pain, to keep her as comfortable as possible." He tucked his glasses in the breast pocket of his white coat and leaned forward, elbows on his knees, hands clasped in front. "I'm sorry, but there is nothing else we can do."

He let those words sink in before he went on. "If you have any out of town relatives or friends who'd like to make a visit, you should call and tell them to stop by to see her . . . sometime today."

Dr. Tolbert crossed the room to exit, but paused with his hand on the doorknob. "I am so sorry. Dana is a lovely person." The door closed softly behind him.

Morphine kept Dana comfortable, but in a deep sleep. She came around for a few minutes every couple of hours, sometimes lucid enough to speak and recognize the people in her room. Lisa thought her sister must know her life was drawing to an end, but she wasn't certain. When her time did come, she hoped Dana would be sound asleep, in the midst of a peaceful dream, and never know when she crossed over to the other side.

Lightning flashed outside the room's lone window. Gray clouds had rolled in to mar the sunshine. Not that it made any difference.

Classical music streamed from the CD player on the bedside table. Lisa had brought it back after a trip home for a bath and change of clothes—the only time she'd left the hospital in three days. She had stopped at a music store on the way and picked up some CDs. With no idea which composer Dana liked best, she'd grabbed a few with interesting covers from the classical section. Lisa switched them periodically and set the player to repeat when it came to the end of a disk. She only hoped Dana could hear the music she loved so dearly.

Something else sat on the bedside table. Dana had snatched up a framed photo from her coffee table before rushing to the hospital. Perhaps she'd known this would be her last trip through the emergency room, or maybe she just planned to look at it while she recuperated.

Lisa picked up the frame, then wiped away a tear that trickled down her cheek. She would not allow herself to cry now. Not while she could watch the rise and fall of Dana's chest while she breathed. There would be plenty of time for mourning in the not so distant future, but not now, not yet.

She stared at the landscape taken from the hot air balloon a month earlier and remembered the look of pure joy on Dana's face, an expression that had stayed there the whole time they floated through the clouds, bathed in the rosy glow of sunrise. In the photo, a patch of wildflowers blooming beside the meadow in the early light gave the impression of a magical land the Purcell sisters would have loved to explore during their childhood. Lisa had seen Dana gaze at the picture the previous evening.

Lisa recalled the last time she'd said her final goodbyes, proud she'd been able to make the past six weeks of Dana's life bearable, full of as much living and normalcy as possible. Then, she'd wished she could go back in time and redo the way she'd tiptoed around on eggshells, refusing to let Dana get off the couch for fear death would steal her away the first time she let her guard down. By some miracle, Dana had pulled through, her life extended another month and a half. Good to her word, Lisa had bit her tongue and helped her enjoy herself any way she could.

This time, there was nothing she wanted to go back and change.

Movement on the pillow hinted that Dana was waking up. Her head moved in slow motion from side to side as she licked her parched lips. Lisa bit the inside of her own cheek when she noticed a wave of pain ebb its way across Dana's face. That sweet face she had loved, argued with, and confided in for the past thirty-nine years.

"Lisa," Dana said, slowly opening her eyes. She seemed confused, her mind fuzzy from the pain medications that dripped through the IV. "Is that Mozart's Clarinet Concerto I hear? And you haven't switched it to that loud rock crap you like?" Her voice sounded thick and groggy. "Guess it's my turn to pick."

"Yep, it's your turn to pick." Lisa held Dana's frail hand sandwiched between both of her own.

"I always liked this song." She dipped her head in time to the music for a couple of beats. "Is Galahad here?" Dana visually searched the room for the dog.

"No, he's at home. Probably on the sofa, chewing on one of his toys." Lisa figured the drugs were to blame for Dana's confusion.

Dana winced in pain and clutched at her chest.

"You okay?" Lisa tried to stay calm but urgency permeated her voice. "Want me to get you anything?"

"See if the nurse can give me a shot of morphine. That stuff really helps." Pain flashed in Dana's eyes, replacing the twinkle that once lived there. She forced a weak grin. "I'm gonna be a junkie if I ever get out of this place. Might be fun. Who knows?"

Lisa pushed the call button for the nurse's station and passed on Dana's request for more morphine, which the RN was quick to administer.

"I love you, Lis," Dana said, her eyelids heavy.

Lisa struggled to hold back tears, but made sure Dana saw her smiling down at her before she closed her eyes. "Love you too."

Mercifully, the pain medication worked its magic.

CHAPTER THIRTEEN

Death, the sable smoke where vanishes
the flame.
~ Lord Byron

The morphine eased Dana's pain and she lapsed into a deep sleep while Lisa sat quietly at her side. Soon after, the monitors sounded and flashed.

As the medical team rushed into the room, Lisa kissed her sister on the forehead. Then she ran down the hall to get the rest of her family, so they could all be near Dana, together for the end.

They returned to find Dr. Tolbert beside the bed. Thunder crescendoed as people in white coats and scrubs ushered themselves out of the room and closed the door.

"Dana will stop breathing in a matter of minutes." He turned off the sound on the monitors, but they could still see the jagged line of her heartbeat grow weaker with each pulse. "She's not feeling any pain, thanks to the morphine. She'll pass away peacefully." Dr. Tolbert paused to pat Marcus on the arm, and then slipped into the hall.

"Can I hug her?" Marcus asked. Tears streaked his face. "Will it hurt her if I touch her?" He moved to embrace his mother, but then pulled himself back as if waiting for permission.

Keith sat on the edge of his wife's bed, the same spot Lisa had occupied minutes before. He buried his face in his hands, his back moving in silent, grief-stricken heaves. One hand motioned in a failed gesture. He tried to speak but all that came out of his mouth was a croaked "Marc . . ."

Lisa stepped up. "Of course you can, Marcus." Tears flowed down her cheeks, but that didn't make any difference now. She was determined to keep her voice steady enough to answer Marcus, her loving nephew she'd promised to take care of.

She placed her arm around his trembling shoulders. "I know your mama would like that. You won't hurt her. Go ahead, honey." She stooped to kiss Dana's cheek, whispered "I love you so much" in her ear, and knew it would be the last time.

Lisa gently pulled Marcus forward. "Your mom loves you more than anything in this world."

Marcus half laid himself on the bed, buried his face on his mother's shoulder, and hugged her. The sound of his weeping pierced Lisa's hearts like a butcher knife. Sharon, her face a mask of despair, moved to comfort the boy. Lisa stepped in her path to stop her, then guided her mother to the most comfortable chair in the room. Sharon sank into the upholstery and sobbed.

Megan stood at the foot of the bed, pale as a ghost, biting her lip. Lisa hugged her, then asked if she was okay.

"I want to tell Aunt Dana goodbye," she whispered between sniffles, "but I don't want to get in the way, or say the wrong thing. I just don't want her to go." Megan stared at her mother through wide tear-brimmed eyes, looking much more like a lost child than a twenty-two-year-old woman.

"Come on, sweetheart." Lisa steered her by the shoulders toward the head of the hospital bed, the side across from Marcus. She nudged Megan along, the same as she'd done for her nephew. "Tell her."

Keith glanced up and saw Megan hold back. He nodded toward Dana, then patted Megan on the arm before he rested his head in his hands once again.

Megan muttered something in Dana's ear and kissed her cheek. She turned and stumbled back to the foot of the bed, sobbing openly. Lisa knew her daughter well enough to understand she needed a moment to herself.

Lisa touched Keith's shoulder. He cried harder, his face still averted.

Dana's breathing came slower.

A nerve-shattering pause followed each ragged breath. Finally, mercifully, she inhaled for the last time.

The monitor beside the bed flatlined. Five hearts simultaneously broke.

The family was in a dazed, grief-stricken stupor. They had known this day was coming for months, but each held onto a spark of hope that it wouldn't, that a miracle would happen and Dana would escape death's clutches.

Reprieve had not come this time.

A few members of the medical staff came in to turn off the monitors and such. An orderly shut off the CD player. The soothing flow of classical music stopped abruptly, drowning the room in a cold shroud of silence.

Lisa wondered if she was in the midst of a nightmare, but knew that wasn't the case. Grief gnawed her heart. Never had she felt so alone, so sad and numb.

Rain pelted the window, the drops merging together in tiny rivulets that traced winding paths to the windowsill. Nature's tears; even the sky seemed to mourn Dana's demise.

A nurse spoke to the room in general, asking for someone to fill out the death certificate. Keith seemed relieved when Lisa took the clipboard and pen.

Keith sat beside Marcus, and the two seemed to hold each other up. Sharon and Megan stood in a similar embrace at the foot of the bed.

In the chair she'd slept in the night before last, Lisa propped the clipboard against the armrest. She printed 'Dana Marie Purcell Yager' for the decedent's name, checked off the box labeled female, and so on. Pausing every couple of minutes to wipe tears that blurred her vision, she filled in the mundane details on the form. There was no space for the favorite food of the deceased, the title of her favorite book, or the name of her favorite song. No slot asked about the people Dana Marie Purcell Yager loved the most, or for the names of those crushed by grief over her loss.

∗

At home that night, Lisa placed the CD player on the coffee table before she collapsed on her sofa. She still found it hard to believe Dana was dead. Never again would she answer the phone and hear her sister on the other end of the line, chattering away about the events of the day. Dana's big beautiful brown eyes would never sparkle again in this world. They were closed forever.

Galahad ran to greet Lisa with a lick on her hand. He'd had plenty of food in his dish, and he'd been able to let himself out into the fenced backyard through the doggie door, but it was obvious he'd missed her companionship.

"Not now," Lisa said, waving him away. She loved the dog dearly but was too busy drowning in grief to stop and play.

She looked up later when something landed on her foot. Galahad sat in front of her, his noble head cocked to one side. His tennis ball— the one Dana had thrown for him so many times—now lay at her feet.

"She's gone, boy." Lisa leaned forward to scratch the dog behind his ears. "Our poor Dana has passed away. You'll miss her too, won't you?"

Galahad couldn't have known the meaning behind her words, yet he seemed to comprehend her misery and heartbreak. Lisa hugged Galahad, and her tears would not stop.

CHAPTER FOURTEEN

For death is no more than a turning of us over
from time to eternity.
~William Penn

A steady stream of family, friends, and acquaintances flowed through Murphy's Funeral Home to pay their respects.

The immediate family sat on the front row; Keith and Marcus were on the end nearest the aisle, Sharon next to them, then Lisa and Megan. Sometimes they stared blankly at the floor or at the subtle design in the wallpaper. When not dabbing their eyes with cotton handkerchiefs or gazing at Dana's casket, the bereaved listened to sympathetic words offered by the line of people who passed between them and the coffin.

Lisa grew restless, overcome by the urge to either walk or scream. Twice she had ambled a circuit around the front of the room, pretending to read the cards attached to the beautiful flowers and potted plants.

The funeral arrangements Dana had planned months before made things much easier for the family. They recognized her persnickety style in the small details of the preparations she'd spared them from having to make.

Lisa reached into her purse for the remembrance card taken from a stack on the table in the entranceway. She studied the picture on the front of a bridge in the woods, pink dogwood petals drifting through sunshine reflected in the stream below, a horse drawn carriage in the distance stirring a swirl of dust as it trotted down the lane toward the bridge. She opened the card and read a verse written by Emily Dickinson:

"Because I could not stop for Death,
He kindly stopped for me.
The Carriage held but just ourselves
And Immortality"

'In Loving Memory' headed the page opposite the poem. The words centered below reminded Lisa of the drab facts on the death certificate she'd filled out a few days before.

Dana Marie Purcell Yager
Age Thirty-nine
Daughter of Sharon and the late John Purcell
Wife to Keith and mother of Marcus
Died September 20th at Mercy United Hospital
Funeral held 2 p.m. September 23rd
at Murphy's Funeral Home
Interment to follow in Mount Zion Cemetery
Reverend Larry Baxter, officiating

Mr. Murphy, the funeral director, approached Keith's seat. He knelt beside him, his voice a solemn whisper as he spoke. "The service will start in about two minutes."

Keith nodded, then patted Marcus on the knee.

Elegant violin music wafted into the room, a signal for mourners to cease talking and take their seats. Lisa, twisting a tissue in her clammy hands, recognized the tune as one she'd heard on Dana's car stereo dozens of times. Agony gripped her stomach. She'd never again have the chance to argue about music with her sister.

Reverend Larry Baxter stepped up to the wooden podium, cleared his throat, and started the service. Lisa listened to him speak and decided Dana had chosen the right man. His words focused on Dana's life and sounded nothing like a sermon, just as he'd promised.

Larry read only one scripture, the twenty-third Psalm, which he recited with feeling and reverence. His deep voice threatened to break when he glanced at the girl he'd gone to high school with, now lying in her coffin. "The Lord is my shepherd, I shall not want. He maketh me to lie down in green pastures. He leadeth me beside the still waters. He restoreth my soul. He leadeth me in the paths of righteousness for his name's sake. Yea, though I walk through the valley of the shadow of death, I will fear no evil, for thou art with me. Thy rod and thy staff, they comfort me. Thou preparest a table before me in the presence of mine enemies. Thou anointest my head with oil. My cup runneth over. Surely goodness and mercy shall follow me all the days of my life, and I will dwell in the house of the Lord, forever."

"Amazing Grace" filled the room as Reverend Baxter took his seat behind the podium. The soulful voice that poured from the speakers prompted people to pull Kleenex or hankies from their pockets. Sentimentality, always abundant in a funeral home, overtook the room.

When the song ended, Reverend Baxter once again took his place at the lectern. Lisa stared at the cherry coffin in front of her; her gaze lingered on each detail Dana had painstakingly selected, from the silky smooth pink lining to the ornate carving on the corners. Someone, the undertaker or maybe a cosmetologist, had done a nice job on Dana's hair and make-up. She looked so natural, more as she had before her health deteriorated. Lisa guessed the navy suit's extra fabric was pinned in the back, since Dana had lost so much more weight after the alterations.

She turned her attention back to Larry Baxter. " . . . so Dana wanted to have this next song played today as a dedication to her family, as another way to tell them how much she loved them, and felt loved by them. Her eyes would just light up with joy when she spoke of her family. So this song is for Keith, her loving husband of twenty years. For Marcus, her son and the light of her life. For Lisa, her big sister and the best friend she ever knew. For Megan, the niece that was like a daughter to her. And this song is for Sharon, Dana's loving mother." As the minister seated himself behind the platform, music started to play.

A lump rose in Lisa's throat when she heard "Have I Told You Lately That I Love You" by Rod Stewart. Her mind flashed to a time she'd sang along to it driving down the highway, Dana laughing beside her, threatening to change the station. Lisa knew Dana had chosen this song for her today. Rod Stewart's voice was sultry velvet as he sang about a loved one who eases trouble and chases sadness away. The very things she'd tried her best to do for sister, especially these last few weeks.

During the second chorus of the song, Lisa's broken heart ripped open the emotional floodgates she'd kept locked away for so long. She wept in loud, gut-wrenching sobs. Beside her, Sharon and Megan did the only thing they could. Sandwiching her between them, their arms twined around her, they melted into an emotional heap of sorrow.

Reverend Baxter took his time getting back on his feet after the ballad's final notes, to give the family a minute to compose themselves.

"There is one more thing Dana made me promise to do for her today." He reached underneath the podium and pulled out a picture frame, then placed it in a position of honor on the table to his left. A cloth draped over the front hid the picture from view.

"If you knew Dana, you know she liked having things her way. Well, God bless her, she didn't think today ought to be any different. This," Rev. Baxter said as he removed the cloth to reveal what was underneath, "is how Dana wanted us to remember her."

Dana smiled at them from the photograph, her face full, her brown eyes twinkling with almost as much mischief as the day she'd made Lisa try on that hellaciously ugly dress with the matching hat. Lisa had no idea when she'd had this picture taken, but guessed it was soon after that shopping trip. Dana had posed in the same navy suit and frilly pink blouse she wore now, in the coffin.

Reverend Baxter continued, "She knew you all would be sad today, but she wanted everyone to leave here knowing she loved you. The final song she selected is definitely *not* what you normally hear at a funeral, but it was her favorite, and, you know Dana, she insisted." He signaled for the music.

"She wanted everyone to look at this picture while you listen to Beethoven's 'Ode to Joy', and remember a special time you shared with her." A tear rolled down the minister's face. "Dana said she dares you not to smile."

Joyful music filled the room. All eyes were glued to the photograph. Dana's wish came true; most people took the dare and smiled in spite of themselves as they wept. The five people seated on the front row were lost in memories and tears.

The room fell silent when the song and the service drew to an end, a fitting tribute to the life of Dana Yager.

Lisa would not leave her seat until she watched the funeral director keep the promise he'd made to her that morning.

Before he closed the coffin, Mr. Murphy unpinned the small bouquet of rosebuds from its spot inside the lid, and gently placed it in Dana's hand.

CHAPTER FIFTEEN

Gaily I lived as ease and nature taught,
And spent my little life without a thought,
And am amazed that Death, that tyrant grim,
Should think of me, who never thought of him.
~ René Francois Regnier

The reading of the will was held on October forth, two weeks after Dana's final breath. The things she had bequeathed to her relatives weren't of a monetary nature, since her assets reverted to Keith and Marcus. She left short notes to the ones she loved the most, along with keepsakes that would have a special place in their hearts.

A lawyer handed out envelopes and gift-wrapped packages to Keith, Marcus, Sharon,

Lisa, and Megan. They decided to read the letters silently to themselves while they were all together, but to wait and open their gifts in private.

In her letter to Lisa, Dana told her how much she treasured the time they spent together and that she loved her. The passage about the balloon ride touched Lisa's heart the most. Tears coursed down her face as she read Dana's neat curlicue script:

I can't express in words how much the hot air balloon ride meant to me, or how much I appreciate it. First, I have to fuss at you for spending way too much money on me. I know because I looked up what it cost on the internet. Are you crazy! It was too much, but I'm so glad you did it. I absolutely loved every single second of it. Thanks, Lis!

Secondly, I need to let you know why the flight was so

significant for me. I felt safe and free up there, everything was so beautiful and perfect. There was a moment, up there in the clouds, when I quit fearing death. I know it may sound silly, but it was the horizon, with the sun warm and pink all around us. It was a new day being born out of the darkness. I realized right then that wherever it is I'm destined to go after I die, it's not the end of me. It's going to be the beginning of the next phase of my existence. I'm not sure exactly what will be waiting for me, but I feel in my heart it will be as beautiful as that sunrise.

Back at home that afternoon, Galahad followed Lisa out to the patio. She set the three wrapped packages down on a wicker chair and uncorked a chilled bottle of Chardonnay. She was just beginning to comprehend that her sister was gone, pain free and at peace. After savoring half a glass of wine, she turned her attention to the gifts.

She contemplated the pile of carefully wrapped presents, then decided to start with the largest and work her way down. The first one was big and flat. The polka-dotted paper pulled away to unveil a framed landscape, a painting of the photo taken from the hot air balloon, the sunrise over a field of wildflowers. It was beautiful. Lisa knew just the spot to hang it—in her living room where she could enjoy it every day. Each time she saw it, she'd feel Dana's love shining through the pink horizon.

The next package was the size of a boot box and rattled when Lisa shook it. She opened the lid and laughed, then lifted out a huge red monkey. A yellow Post-it note stuck to its belly proclaimed 'For Galahad!' in big blue letters.

Lisa showed the German shepherd his present. He sniffed the stuffed monkey and must have picked up Dana's scent. His tail wagged as he scanned the backyard, perhaps trying to find someone who now lived in a loftier place, one as beautiful and warm as a glowing pink sunrise. Galahad's head tilted sideways, confused for a second. Then he picked up his new toy and ran laps around the lawn with it.

Lisa wiped her eyes with her sleeve and reached for the third gift. "The best things always come in small packages."

The necklace she found within was exquisite, an oval locket made of antique gold. Inside, on the left, was a close-up of Dana's beautiful face, her eyes sparkling and full of life. The right side held a picture of two little girls, one about four, the other about eight years old.

The Purcell sisters, little Dana and Big Sis Lisa, holding hands for eternity.

About the Author

Photo courtesy of Brittany Hayes

Tina D.C. Hayes writes romantic suspense and cozy mysteries. She lives in western Kentucky with her husband and three children. A few pampered pooches and two parrots keep her busy, but guard against writer's block.

http://tinadchayes.wordpress.com
http://twitter.com/Tina_DC_Hayes